THE Little Goat ON THE ROOF

SKANDISK, INC.

MINNEAPOLIS, MINNESOTA 55438

THE LITTLE GOAT ON THE ROOF

Published by Skandisk, Inc. 1998
Skandisk, Inc.
6667 West Old Shakopee Road, Suite 109
Bloomington, MN 55438

ISBN 1-57534-029-1

Printed in the United States of America

Skandisk, Inc., publishes *The Tomten,* a catalog which offers
exemplary children's literature, immigrant books, Scandinavian literature,
music and gifts with a Scandinavian accent.

For more information write to The Tomten,
6667 West Old Shakopee Road, Suite 109
Bloomington, MN 55438

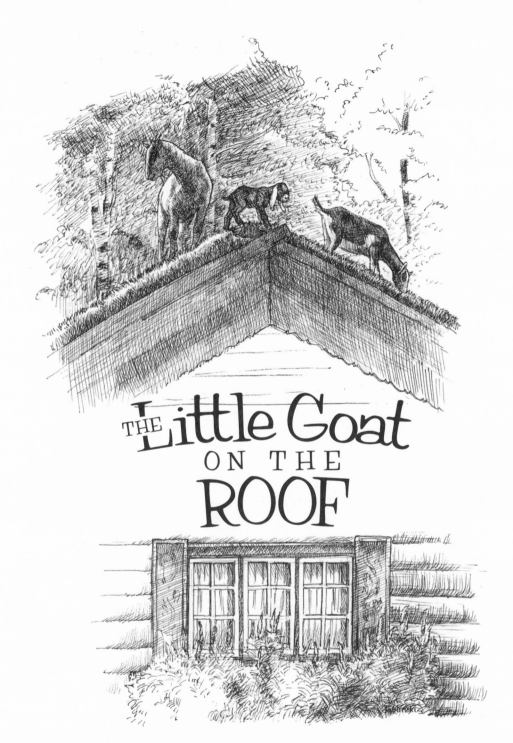

The Little Goat
ON THE
ROOF

JODY LITTLER
Illustrated by JAN JABLONSKI

It's springtime again in Door County.

The grass is green, the sun is warm, and it is time for the goats to go back up on the roof of Al Johnson's Swedish Restaurant! It is an exciting time for everyone, but especially for a little goat named "DeeCee." Life on the roof is a world of wonder and adventure!

My name is DeeCee and this is my mother, Nanny. I was born in a cozy straw-filled barn. Nanny and I live there with many other goats: nannies, billies, and kids just like me.

Nanny tells me we are special goats because of the work we do for Mr. Al Johnson. She whispers in my ear that I am also a lucky little goat, because I was born in a very important year!

Many times in the barn, I heard the older goats talk about the "newest kid" at Al's, and how happy it made Al. I just knew they were talking about me. It felt good to be loved and fussed over. In my heart, I knew I must be Al's favorite kid if I made him so happy. I would hold my head up high and scamper away! Only sometimes I would forget to watch where I was going!

My Nanny explained to me that we live in a village called Sister Bay in Door County, Wisconsin. My name DeeCee is short for Door County. My owners, Al and his wife Ingert, are well-known because of their business. In the restaurant, they serve Swedish pancakes that are square and paper thin and meatballs that are round! So many times, from up on the roof, I can smell the good food cooking below. I wonder what those pancakes and meatballs would taste like, on a bed of grass of course!

Most goats live on farms all their lives where they graze in fields all day and sleep in barns at night. But not Al's goats! A truck comes for us every morning, and we climb in the back of the pick-up and go for a ride into Sister Bay. Our truck has high sides on it so we don't jump out, but I'm too scared to jump anyway. I just stay close to my Nanny and another kid named Bo. Bo was also born this spring, so we play together a lot. As the truck leaves the farm, I pretend to be so tall that I can see all the wide open fields around me.

If I look over the truck hood, I can see water up ahead.
I would run straight into it, kick up my hooves and splash all
the Billy goats if I could! Now we go down a big hill, weeeeh!
My feet wobble a bit, I lean into Nanny to catch my balance!
As we round the corner, we pass car after car after car.
I look for a kid like me in each car. My head swings back
and forth so fast that I get dizzy and lose my footing all over again!

I get up just in time to see all
the boats at the Marina, and I know
we are almost to our second home, the
roof at Al Johnson's Swedish Restaurant!

The truck takes us around the back of the building to the big
wooden ramp made especially for us. The bigger goats climb right up, but I love to be
carried up the steps by one of the big guys that drives our truck!

At the top of the ramp is our grassy playground! Bo and I butt heads, kick up our heels, and chase each other all over our playground.

We eat the long grass when we are hungry and lie down to rest when we are tired!

I put my head down on the soft grass,
close my eyes, and dream of . . . sneaking down the
brown wooden ramp and trotting up and down the streets
of town. I run past the Post Office, past several little
shops, and part way up the big hill before I stop and catch
my breath. Then I turn and run down the hill so fast I feel
like I am flying! I gallop so fast that I am already back by
the front door of the restaurant. I've always wondered
what is behind those big wooden doors. Everyone is so
busy; no one seems to be watching me. Now is my
chance to see the inside of the building! I sneak in the
doors between a big person's legs.

Once inside, I look both ways, but follow my nose toward the good smells coming from the kitchen. I scamper past the hostess, who is busy seating people. I'm in the dining room! I look around. It is a big room with many people sitting at tables and some others moving around with big trays of food. I spot an empty seat. I run and jump up into it wishing for a tasty treat, only to come sliding off the chair to land, kerplunk, on the floor.

Just then, I spot Al coming out from the kitchen and I head for the front door before he sees me! Out front, I run past the big windows, around the building and up the ramp . . . just as I wake up and hear Al calling, "DeeCee, come on boy; it's time to go back to the farm."

Sometimes when I am not sleeping or munching grass, I lie and wonder why the truck picks us up every day to take us to the big roof to play?! One day when I was lying down close to the edge of the roof, I peeked over and saw that there were people looking back up at me! I was so surprised! I looked again, and sure enough, they were still there, smiling and pointing up at me! I ran to tell Nanny about the people who were watching me. She just laughed and said that people come to see us every day. If I would pay more attention, I would know that! Now I do pay attention! I go and check often to see who is watching me!

Sometimes, Bo and I run up one peak and down in the little valley and up over the other peak. That way we can see who is looking at us from both sides of our grassy playground. Children about our size are our favorite! They wave at us and smile. Sometimes we baa for them or kick up our heels and play!

My favorite thing is when Al comes up on the roof to be with us. He gives me treats and often carries me down the ramp when it is time to go back to the barn. When he picks me up and carries me, I just know I am his favorite kid!

Then it is back in the truck and off to the barn. Usually one of the truck drivers rides in the back with us. I asked Nanny why he did that, and she said that one goat used to like to jump out of the back of the truck. One time he leaped out and over the tops of some cars in back of us and got away! He ran away to the Sister Bay beach. I have never been to the beach, but Nanny says it is no place for a goat! I guess if I'm going to be Al's favorite kid, I'd better not ever run away to the beach! But I do wonder what sand would feel like on my hooves and what it would taste like!

Sometimes at night in the barn, the older goats like to tell stories. Oscar was the first goat to ever go up on Al's roof. The story is that he was given to Al by his friend Winkie. Winkie was always playing tricks on Al and one day Al caught him trying to carry Oscar up the ladder and onto the roof. But . . . instead of getting him on top of the roof, Oscar wiggled and wiggled and knocked Winkie right off the ladder. They both ended up on the ground! Oscar wasn't hurt, but Winkie broke his collarbone. Not one to give up easily, Winkie did find a way to get Oscar up on the roof to stay . . . and so all of us little goats need to have his legend passed on to us.

Sometimes the oldest goats tell stories passed down to them of "the old country". They tell me it is so beautiful over there with lots of green grass and flowers. People used to build their houses into the sides of hills and all the animals grazed on the grass that grew there. They tell me that the logs for the restaurant and the smaller buildings came from Norway. But I think the grass came from here! I guess there were many grass-roofed houses in Norway and Sweden where goats could graze, but Al's grass roof is the only one I have found in Sister Bay! And if I'm going to stay Al's favorite kid, I'd better not try to find the "old" country!

When some of the oldest goats talk about how great it must have been over there, the younger billy goats remind them that we have the best world of all! When it is nice and warm outside, we get to be with all the people and when it is cold and rainy, we get to be warm inside the barn.

Nanny tells me that people buy pictures, called postcards, of us in the place under our grassy playground. Then they send them to their friends back home. People come from far away to see Al and his wife Ingert, because their restaurant is famous. Nanny explained that we are famous, too. I am not sure I understand it all, but it is ok with me if Al and I are famous, as long as I am still his favorite kid!

Nanny smiled and quietly told me never to say that aloud, because I wasn't Al's only favorite kid. She said someone was born this year that changed all that! That's what made this year so special. I was pretty sleepy and was not sure I had heard my Nanny right. I fell asleep that night dreaming about Al carrying me up on the roof . . .

The next day, as I was peeking over the front edge of the roof, I saw Al come out carrying a little boy. People were crowding around to see him. I could hear Al saying, "This is my little Bjorn, my favorite grandkid!" I looked and listened and could not believe what I was hearing! What was he saying about his favorite?

Just then, Nanny walked over by me, whispered in my ear and said, "The little one was born earlier this year, just like you. He is Bjorn, the Johnson's first grandchild! Look, isn't he sweet? He looks just like his grandpa!

I had to agree with Nanny; he was awfully sweet. As I stood and looked at him, he pointed up at me and smiled! Al looked up at me and smiled, too! And I finally understood . . . Bjorn was Al's favorite grandkid, but I could still be his favorite goatkid! Nanny was right, I was born in a lucky year, and we are special goats . . . the goats of Al Johnson's roof!

That night, when I snuggled down in the straw, I fell asleep dreaming. I dreamt that Bjorn had grown into a playful young boy. Together we scampered around on the big grassy playground on the roof. We would always be Al's favorite kids.

THE END

JODY LITTLER grew up in Sister Bay, Wisconsin.
She fondly remembers eating at Al Johnson's.
Drawing from her childhood experience she has written
a charming tale set at Door County's popular landmark,
Al Johnson's Swedish Restaurant.

JAN M. JABLONSKI, resides in Door County
and applies her artistic talent to doing portraits and
landscapes, and sometimes goats, as well as dollmaking.